Bio-pirate

Michele Martin Bossley

Orca currents

ORCA BOOK PUBLISHERS

To my son Andrew...a true miracle.

Library and Archives Canada Cataloguing in Publication

Bossley, Michele Martin

Bio-pirate / written by Michele Martin Bossley.
(Orca currents)

ISBN 978-1-55143-895-5 (bound).--ISBN 978-1-55143-893-1 (pbk.)

I. Title. II. Series.
PS8553.O7394B56 2008   jC813'.54   C2008-903391-4

Summary: Three amateur sleuths learn about biological piracy in
their pursuit of stolen research.

First published in the United States, 2008
Library of Congress Control Number: 2008929299

Orca Book Publishers gratefully acknowledges the support for its publishing
programs provided by the following agencies: the Government of Canada
through the Book Publishing Industry Development Program and the
Canada Council for the Arts, and the Province of British Columbia
through the BC Arts Council and the Book Publishing Tax Credit.

Cover design by Teresa Bubela
Cover photography by Dreamstime

Orca Book Publishers
PO Box 5626, Station B
Victoria, BC Canada
V8R 6S4

Orca Book Publishers
PO Box 468
Custer, WA USA
98240-0468

www.orcabook.com
Printed and bound in Canada.
Printed on 100% PCW recycled paper.

11 10 09 08 • 4 3 2 1

chapter one

"Hey! Look at this," I called. "It works." I steered my robot around an apple core I'd placed on the floor.

"Way to go, Trev," Nick said as the robot ran over the apple core, smearing apple mush across the floor.

I shook the controls. "It's not as easy as it looks." The robot tipped over and lay there, whirring on the floor.

"This is all such garbage," Nola said, disgusted. "I thought we were going to actually learn something in this course."

"You don't call programming a robot to figure out a maze learning something?" Robyn bristled.

"No. I meant something more...important," Nola said.

"This camp is supposed to be fun," I said.

My cousin Nick, our friend Robyn and I were spending part of summer vacation at the University of Calgary. Our parents figured we'd had enough TV, video games and loafing in the sun, so they stuck us in a university day camp. It was cool, actually. We used computers to program robots, learned how to use electricity to build a minicar and a bunch of other neat stuff. The only drawback was Nola, one of the girls in the camp. She was way too smart—a total know-it-all. She was even worse than Robyn.

"You guys are so lame," Nola snorted. "You just don't get it, do you? We're here at a major medical research facility and we're playing with robots?"

"You were expecting maybe to work on

your master's thesis?" Robyn said. "Come on, Nola. You're only in grade eight."

"So?" Nola said. "I can still be interested, can't I? These people are looking for the cure for cancer. There are all kinds of discoveries being made here."

"She's right." Meredith, one of our instructors, overheard Nola's last comment and paused in her circuit of the room. "There's some fantastic research being done at this university. I'm hoping to be accepted here as a graduate student."

"You don't go to school here?" I asked, surprised.

"Not anymore. I did my undergraduate degree here, but I've been working for a company that's involved with research work in the Faculty of Medicine." She smiled at us.

"What kind of research?" Nola asked.

"Well, I'm not involved in the big stuff, but the university does everything from testing new treatments and drugs to developing new medical procedures."

"But what kinds of drugs and treatments?" Nola persisted.

Meredith frowned. "Well, I can't really say. That information is kept private until the university is ready to release it."

"You mean it's kept a secret!" Nola said with some fire.

The instructor looked at her in surprise. "Well, we can't tell people that a pill derived from the earwax of llamas cures acne, unless we know for sure that it works, right?"

"No, but there are other reasons things are covered up," Nola said.

The instructor frowned. "You think so, do you?"

"Look, I know the kind of stuff that goes on. People don't always play by the rules, you know." Nola frowned. "I've read about cases where research teams learn about ancient medicines from third world countries. Then they take out patents on those remedies."

"So?" Robyn raised her eyebrows.

"So," Nola said, "that means no one else in the world can legally produce those medicines. The researchers sell them for huge money to big corporate drug companies. They're only interested in getting rich."

"That might be true, but I can assure you that the university's policy has more to do with public safety than biological piracy," said Meredith. "Maybe you should think about what you're saying."

Undaunted, Nola eyed her calmly. "I do."

Meredith shook her head and moved on to the next group of kids. Nola turned her attention back to her computer.

"What was that all about?" I whispered to Robyn. I tinkered with the wires on the back of the robot, trying to correct the steering problem. Robyn just shrugged.

"I have no idea," she said. She twisted an elastic band around her ponytail and pulled it tight. Tall, athletic and freckled, Robyn didn't usually take guff from anyone. I was surprised Robyn had actually let Nola sound off like she had.

Does earwax from a llama really cure acne?" Nick asked, thoughtfully rubbing a zit on his chin.

"No, doofus!" Robyn said. "That was just an example!"

"How do you know?" Nick demanded, as I steered my robot along the floor. "Maybe she just let top secret research out of the bag." He shifted his lanky body, trying to find a comfortable spot for his long legs under the desk.

"Get real!" Robyn said.

I let out a yelp as sparks emitted from the back of my robot. "Help! It's on fire!" I fanned the smoking machinery with my ball cap.

"Stop! You're making it worse," Robyn yelled. "We need a fire extinguisher!"

A spark landed on my cap and a fresh flame caught hold. I beat it against the tile floor. It was my favorite hat, and I wasn't going to let it go without a fight.

"Look out!" Meredith yelled, as the robot exploded in a spray of metal parts. She barreled through the group, carrying a fire extinguisher. She pulled the pin and spewed foam everywhere. In a matter of seconds, the lab was covered in a thick layer of white.

Everyone relaxed. But then the smoke alarm went off. The horrible clang was deafening. Most of the class clutched their hands over their ears.

"Rats!" Meredith looked like she wanted to say something much worse, but she managed to control the urge. "We have to evacuate the building, kids."

"But the fire's out," Robyn shouted above the persistent jangle of the alarm.

"It doesn't matter!" Meredith hollered back. "It's procedure. Everyone get in line and follow me. The fire exit is through my office. No one is to use the elevator, understand?"

We filed through the office area past the lab. Last in line and still clutching my ball cap, I brushed past mountains of papers and books on Meredith's desk. The edge of a bright yellow file folder caught on my jeans and slipped to the floor, spilling the contents.

"That's just great," I muttered. I scooped up the handwritten notes and tucked them back in the file, then shoved the yellow folder back under the piles of paper on the desk. I realized that if the fire had spread, this whole office would have gone up in flames. Any research that was being done here would have been lost.

It had only been seconds, but I glanced up and realized that I was alone in the office. The rest of the class had already reached the stairwell.

A pair of eyeballs peered over the edge of the desk. I froze in shock.

They were human eyeballs...that were still attached to a human head.

I suppressed the urge to yell as a guy popped up from behind a desk and started toward me. Something metal gleamed in one hand. He had a scruffy goatee, a nose ring and a tattoo on his upper arm.

The spit in my mouth dried instantly. My feet were moving before my brain gave the command to run. I sped out of the office and down the stairs, slamming the door behind me.

Breathless, I caught up to Nick and Robyn on the lawn.

"Where were you?" Robyn asked.

I looked, but I could see no sign of Tattoo Guy. "Tell you later," I whispered, as the wail of sirens reached us. The fire trucks roared up to the building, lights flashing.

"Oh, no!" I shoved my ball cap on my head, the visor pulled low.

Nola viewed me with amusement. "That hat has a hole burnt in it," she said.

"I know," I answered. "I don't care."

"It's a Calgary Flames hat, so it kind of works...you know, flames, fire," Robyn offered.

"Ha, ha," I answered glumly.

Nick clapped me on the shoulder. "Hey, don't worry about it, man. But I'll tell you one thing," he said, as the firefighters leaped out of the truck.

"What's that?" I asked.

"You sure do know how to liven up summer camp!"

chapter two

Nick hung up his cell phone. "There's no answer."

"Are you *sure* your mom isn't picking us up?" I asked Robyn, wiping the sweat off my forehead. The late afternoon sun scorched the pavement. Waves of heat shimmered on the black parking lot.

"Positive." Robyn shook her head. "She told me she was driving out of town to go antique shopping with my aunt. I was supposed to wait for them at home."

The three of us were waiting for our ride home. After twenty sweltering minutes and no parents, we'd finally figured out that there had been a mix-up.

"Well, that stinks," Nick said. "It's going to take over an hour to get home on the bus, and I'm dying of heatstroke. How could your mom forget that it was her carpool day?"

Robyn shrugged. Before she could answer, Nola walked by with a tall older man. His graying hair didn't seem to match his smooth brown skin, but his expression was exactly like Nola's.

"Hey, guys," she said. "What are you still doing here?"

"Waiting for a ride that's not coming," Robyn said sourly. "Why are you still here?"

"I was waiting for my dad. He's a professor at this university." She glanced at her father, who smiled and held out his hand. I shook it, feeling a little embarrassed.

"Dr. Pierce," he said. "I teach in the Faculty of Medicine."

"Hi," I answered. "I'm Trevor, and this is Robyn and Nick. We're in the summer day camp with Nola."

"Do you guys need a ride?" Nola asked.

The three of us shared a doubtful glance. Nola was not exactly our favorite person. "We live way down in the south part of the city," I said. "It's a long way from here."

"That's okay, right, Dad? We live in the south too," Nola answered.

"Absolutely. I don't think we should leave you stranded up here when I'm driving that way anyway," Dr. Pierce said. "We can call your parents at work and let them know who I am and that you're fine."

"Well, if you're sure you don't mind...," Robyn trailed off.

"Of course not. Let's go!" Nola led the way to the parkade while Robyn called her dad's office. After her dad talked to Dr. Pierce, we clambered inside their minivan. Dr. Pierce pulled out of the parking stall, and we all relaxed as the air conditioning kicked in.

"I can't believe Meredith, can you?" Nola said, once the van had hit the main roadway. "I mean, really. She was so snotty today, don't you think?"

"Um, well," I said.

"The thing is I'm totally right about this. Bio-piracy is a real issue, and it needs to stop. I'm thinking about organizing a rally."

"Uh, not to sound stupid or anything," Robyn said. "But what exactly are you talking about? What is bio-piracy?"

"I already told you. Weren't you listening?" Nola snapped. "It's when selfish researchers take natural resources and information about traditional remedies from people in developing countries. Big drug companies market the medicines for tons of cash, and then the people who made the medicines in the first place don't get anything."

Dr. Pierce held up his hand. "Nola, you know I agree with you. There have been some terrible instances where people have been taken advantage of. But most research is done for the public good. You need to be careful about these accusations."

Nola just frowned.

I cleared my throat and changed the subject. "So, uh, Dr. Pierce...," I began. "Have you been teaching at the university for very long?"

"More than fifteen years, now. I've seen a lot of changes, that's for sure."

"You mean to the campus?" Robyn asked.

"Well, that too," Dr. Pierce admitted. "But no, I mean to the advances in medical science. The research is fascinating."

"Must be," muttered Nick. Robyn gave him a sharp elbow to the ribs.

"Is it difficult, sir?" she asked.

Dr. Pierce glanced at her through the rearview mirror. "Sometimes. It takes a great deal of perseverance. Why? Are you considering a career in the medical field?"

"Uh, I'm not really sure yet," Robyn answered. "But maybe."

"Well, you have to work very hard and be prepared for setbacks along the way. Sometimes things happen that aren't your fault, but you just have to deal with them anyway." Dr. Pierce scowled at the road in front of him.

"Sounds like something went wrong today," Nola said.

Her father sighed. "One of our doctoral students has been experimenting with a new plant-derived drug that affected certain cancer cells. It was very promising research, but some of the notes have gone missing, and obviously it's very difficult to replicate."

"Where were the plants from this time?" Nola sat up and glared at her father. "And how much more will you have to get in order to redo the research?"

"Nola, please," Dr. Pierce said. "It's been a long day, and the last thing I want is to get into a debate over this again."

"How do you lose important research?" I asked in disbelief.

"I don't know. How do you kids lose your homework?" Dr. Pierce managed to grin at us.

I shrugged. "Homework isn't as important as research."

"That depends. Maybe someday, your homework will be research." Dr. Pierce pulled the van into my driveway. "But maybe in this case, the notes have just been misplaced and will turn up soon. I sure hope so, because this could turn out to be a very important discovery."

The three of us gathered up our stuff and began to get out of the van.

"Wait, you guys," Nola said. "Isn't this Trevor's house? We can still drive Nick and Robyn home."

"I'm staying at Trevor's for dinner," answered Nick.

"And I don't live too far from here," Robyn said. "The boys can walk me home."

"Are you sure?" Dr. Pierce peered at us from over the top of his glasses.

"Yes. Thanks for the ride!" Robyn waved as Dr. Pierce backed out of the driveway.

"What's the big idea?" Nick said. "You live six blocks from here, and it's boiling hot out! The only place I want to walk is straight into the sprinkler!"

"Don't be such a wimp," Robyn said,

striding down the sidewalk. "I wanted to talk to you guys about Nola."

"There is such a thing as a phone," Nick grumbled as we followed her. "Inside, where it's cool."

"What do you think is going on with her?" Robyn ignored Nick.

"She's a wingnut," muttered Nick.

Robyn looked at me. I considered my words carefully. We'd only known Nola for a week. "She's a bit...radical, maybe," I said.

"I think it's weird that she keeps bringing up this bio-piracy thing. What's up with that?" Robyn said.

I shrugged. "She's pretty scrappy. Maybe she just likes to have an argument to support."

"I think it's more than that. I bet Nola is always bugging her dad about using plants in his research. She just doesn't seem to want to let it go."

"Maybe." Perspiration dripped down my forehead, and my T-shirt was sticking to me. "Can we just forget about Nola?" I said. "I'm melting here. I need a pool."

"Me too. But I'll be in one in about two hours," Nick commented.

"What?" I asked.

"I made the cut for the university swim club. They've asked me to join their summer training. If I can keep up with the other swimmers, I could be training there for the rest of the year."

"No way!" Robyn said.

If Nick's face could have gotten any redder, it would have. Nick was the least athletic among us. "Yes way," he said defensively.

"But Nick, you must be really good," said Robyn. "Nola just told me that some of the best swimmers in the city train at that pool."

"Maybe because she trains there," Nick answered glumly. "That's one of the drawbacks."

"Oh." Robyn was silent for a moment.

"Well, congrats, man," I told him. "Aside from Nola, that's great."

"Yeah, maybe." Nick's voice lacked certainty. "My parents want me to try it, but it's big-time practicing. We swim twice a day—first thing in the morning and then again later. I have to be at the pool almost every day. I don't know if I'll like it."

We reached the grassy area near Robyn's house and walked along the chain-link fence that divided the park from the backyards of the houses that bordered it. Some people had planted hedges and trees for privacy, but as we walked past one house, we could see right into the yard.

A guy was carrying a computer into the basement of the house. File boxes, a big desk and an open box filled with jars, beakers and a variety of equipment sat on the lawn.

I paused for a second look, but the guy came back outside. His hair was hidden under a ball cap, and he had a scraggly brown goatee. He bent down to pick up a file box that was obviously heavy, because his biceps bulged under the strain. A thin tattoo ran along his upper arm.

I yanked Nick down and joined Robyn beside a hedge.

"That's the guy from the university!" I whispered. "He was in Meredith's office when my robot blew up."

Robyn gave me a puzzled look. "What guy?"

"Tattoo Guy. I told you about him. The one who was hiding behind Meredith's desk."

Robyn peered through the hedge. "Are you sure?"

"I'm sure," I said. "The tattoo's a dead giveaway."

Robyn studied him through the fence. "So, what's he doing here?" she asked.

"Maybe he lives here," said Nick.

"Well, he's definitely moving in," Robyn observed. "But it looks more like he's planning to set up a laboratory than a bedroom suite. And look what's written on the side of that file box." She pointed at the last cardboard container still on the grass.

I looked. It said *Faculty of Medicine*.

"So what?" Nick said. "We already know he's been at the university."

"Exactly." Robyn pointed her finger at the boxes. "Don't you remember what Dr. Pierce was just telling us about the lost cancer research? What if that's it? Why is all that stuff here if it belongs to the university?"

"Oh, come on, Robyn," Nick scoffed. "What are the odds that this guy is connected to the missing research? There are a ton of people at the university. Besides, Dr. Pierce thinks that research was just misplaced."

Tattoo Guy came outside and picked up the final box. When he straightened up, he stared right at the bush where we were hiding. I knew he saw us. I froze.

Tattoo Guy walked slowly toward the hedge. I tensed. "All right," he growled. "Come out of there!"

"Run!" I said, yanking Robyn to her feet. Nick sprinted after us, toward Robyn's house.

"Come back here!" Tattoo Guy hollered. But by the time he reached the hedge, we were gone.

chapter three

"Let's go, Nick!" Nola shouted from the side of the pool. She tossed him a flutterboard and then jumped into the water herself.

Nick adjusted his goggles and took off, his legs churning a wake behind him. But it didn't matter how fast he kicked—Nola was always right behind him.

Robyn and I were sitting on the bleachers of the pool deck, watching Nick. The best I could figure out, it was organized chaos in the pool. There must have been fifty swimmers in one half of the pool, and they were all traveling at different speeds and doing different things. Nick's group appeared to be doing some kind of relay.

"I don't understand how we got roped into this," Robyn complained. "Nick mentioned pizza, and the next thing I knew, we were on the bus to the university."

"Anytime Nick wants to offer pizza after swim practice, I'm there."

"Yeah, but I wanted to see what Tattoo Guy was up to today," said Robyn. "Saturday is the only day we can check him out, since we're stuck in camp all week. It's been three days since we saw him moving all that stuff into that house."

I glanced at her. "And how were you going to check him out? Ring the doorbell, pretend to sell chocolate bars and then interrogate him?"

Robyn looked thoughtful. "You know, that's not a bad idea."

I groaned. "Robyn, give me a break. The guy is serious trouble. You can tell by looking at him that he's someone we don't want to mess with."

"Trevor, he's up to something. I know it. We can't sit back and do nothing...," Robyn trailed off as Nola's voice rose above the noise of the swimmers.

"Look, Nick, if you can't get the rules straight, you shouldn't be here!" she yelled. Red-faced, she threw her flutterboard up on the deck. Nick was standing up, shaking the water out of his goggles. "Swimmers stay on the right side of the lane. You don't block someone from passing by swimming in the middle."

"I wasn't—" Nick protested.

"Yeah, you were." Nola was obviously furious. "And because you're such a buttbrain, I crashed into Braden and practically got a concussion. Next time, stay on your own side."

"Listen—" Nick began to get angry.

"No, you listen," Nola said. "This team is for people who are here to work. If you're here to show off or mess around, then go somewhere else!" Nola slipped her goggles over her face and dove in to begin the next set of lengths.

Nick glanced over at us, his face pink with embarrassment.

"What's her problem?" Robyn said.

I shrugged. "Who knows? Sounds like she doesn't want Nick on the team."

"Let's go outside for a while," Robyn said in a low voice. "I think Nick should concentrate on his swimming." We climbed down from the bleachers and slipped outside.

The swimming pool was located inside the Kinesiology building on the campus. Robyn and I walked down the hall.

"Pay attention to where we're going," I advised. "We could get lost."

We toured the building, checking out the weight rooms and gyms, the indoor track and the outdoor equipment rental office. There were students everywhere. They were taller than us and were carrying more books, but they were still students.

"Nick's practice is almost over. Maybe we should go back," said Robyn.

I led the way, but I must have made a wrong turn, because we ended up near the speed-skating arena.

"This isn't right," said Robyn.

"Let's try the stairs."

"But we didn't come up any stairs," Robyn said.

"Yeah, I know. But maybe we'll find a more direct way back."

"Or get even more lost," Robyn grumbled. But she followed me.

We passed a row of lockers. It seemed like we were going in the right direction, but then the hallway began to look almost deserted.

"This is kind of creepy," Robyn said.

I had to agree. "Let's go." I turned around and headed back the way we came. Robyn tugged on my sleeve.

"Trevor, I think this is wrong. Didn't we take that hallway?"

I blinked. They all looked the same. "I thought we turned right after the stairs."

"No, it was left," Robyn said.

"I'm sure it was right," I insisted.

We stared at each other.

"Okay, it doesn't matter. We just need to find a staircase and get back on the main level. Then we can ask someone how to get to the pool," I reasoned.

"All right," Robyn agreed. We started off again, but after a few moments, Robyn grabbed my sleeve again.

"What?" I said irritably.

"Look." She pointed to a red backpack lying on the floor near the wall. The contents were scattered all over the floor. The zipper, which had been locked with a tiny padlock, was still closed. Instead, the material had been slashed open—wisps of nylon thread trailed from the opening. A small knife with a jagged edge lay nearby.

I whistled through my teeth. "Somebody meant business."

Robyn began gathering up the pile of belongings.

"What are you doing?" I asked.

"We can't just leave it like this. We need to see who this belongs to, so we can return it," Robyn said. She sifted through the contents.

A screwdriver, a few other small tools and a crumpled business card were scattered on the tile floor. There were no textbooks, only a thin, bright yellow file folder with the words *Faculty of Medicine* scrawled at the top, but no name was visible anywhere. There were several sheets of notepaper with what looked like algebra equations written in messy handwriting. A large envelope marked *CONFIDENTIAL* in red letters was ripped open. It was empty.

I lifted a baggie half-full of small, black round things.

"Eeuuww!" Robyn grimaced. "Are those dried bugs?"

I looked closer, but I couldn't tell what they were. I laid it down carefully. A second baggie full of brownish powder lay partly open. I picked it up gingerly between two fingers.

"What do you suppose this is?" I asked.

"I have no idea, but put it down. What if it's—" Robyn's voice broke off as the bag slipped and the powder spilled everywhere.

"Poison," she finished. We looked at each other in horror through a cloud of brownish dust.

"It smells kind of like chocolate," I said.

Robyn shook the sleeve of her jacket. "It's probably okay," she said nervously. "Just try not to breathe."

I rolled my eyes at her. "Sure, that'll work."

We moved away from the dusty haze. "Why would a student carry around tools?" Robyn pointed at a pair of wire cutters.

"Could be for anything," I said. "We're in the phys-ed area. Maybe they're for fixing sports equipment."

"Okay, but why wouldn't there be more school stuff? Notebooks, textbooks, pens...one file folder is hardly enough for a university class."

I smoothed out the business card that had been on the floor. It was scrunched and fuzzy, like it had been shoved in someone's pocket. "Ever hear of Seaton Pharmaceuticals?"

Robyn shook her head. "Nope." She picked through the film of dust that now lay on the floor and began stuffing the contents back inside the damaged knapsack.

Behind us, the sound of footsteps made us freeze.

chapter four

"Hey!" a voice said.

Robyn and I swung around. I had the business card from the ruined backpack still clenched in my fist. The hallway had been deserted—the voice nearly scared us out of our wits.

It was a woman with blue eyes and glossy dark hair. I recognized her immediately.

"Meredith!"

Her eyes widened at the sight of us. "What are you guys doing down here?"

"We're kind of lost," I admitted. "We're looking for the pool."

"What are you doing with that?" she pointed to the torn backpack and the stuff on the floor.

"We found it," Robyn answered. "Someone vandalized it."

Meredith bent down to scoop the rest of the stuff in the backpack. "Here, give it to me. I'll turn it in to the phys-ed office." She squished the backpack into a ball to hold it together. "Come on. I'll show you the way out."

"Why are *you* down here?" Robyn wanted to know. I sensed the same thing—Meredith seemed to be in a hurry.

Meredith glanced at Robyn with barely concealed irritation. "Some students have lockers down here, you know."

"That doesn't make much sense," Robyn said. "I thought you were in the sciences. Don't you need your books near your classes?"

Meredith laughed. "Well, it doesn't always work out that way. Lockers can be hard to get."

She led us through the corridors, turned several corners and then up a set of stairs. We emerged in a completely different place from where we started.

"Okay. You can get to the pool if you follow this hallway around, take your next right and go through the hallway that leads to the front of the building." Meredith stopped speaking, her face suddenly draining of color. She shoved the backpack at me. "I gotta go."

"Wait!" I called after her. "Where do I turn this in?" But she raced down the hall and didn't answer.

"That's very weird," Robyn said.

I sighed. "Come on. Nick must be done swim practice by now. Maybe he'll know who we give this to."

As we turned to leave, Robyn spotted someone with a halo of wild hair striding toward us. He was carrying an armful of sports equipment and heading toward the Campus Rec office.

"Hey, look," she whispered. "That's Tattoo Guy."

"So? He probably goes to school here," I reasoned.

"Yeah, but maybe that's why Meredith took off. She probably knows him. Maybe she used to be his girlfriend or something," Robyn guessed.

"With that guy?" I asked in disbelief. "He looks like a biker. Not exactly Meredith's type."

Before Robyn could reply, the guy passed us.

He glanced sideways at us and stopped in his tracks. Then he dropped his equipment and strode over.

"Where'd you get this!" he demanded, his eyes on the backpack.

"We...we found it," I stammered.

His jaw tightened. "Where?"

"Downstairs in the basement, hidden in a corner. What's it to you?" Robyn challenged him.

He stared at her in surprise. "Because it's mine, of course."

"Oh, yeah? Prove it." Robyn crossed her arms.

"Robyn, what are you doing?" I whispered. I had the panicked urge to run. This guy looked like a big hairy volcano that was about to explode.

"I want some answers," she said to me. She squared her shoulders and faced Tattoo Guy. "Tell me what was inside," she commanded.

"A yellow file folder jammed with notes, a bio text, some old research papers and, uh...some stuff for an experiment," he answered.

"Wrong!" Robyn sang out. My jaw hung open in disbelief. I expected to be dismembered at any second. She was arguing with the guy like he was her older brother.

"What do you mean, wrong?" he growled. "Look, girlie, this backpack is mine. I shouldn't have to prove anything to you."

"You do if it doesn't really belong to you," Robyn insisted. "This pack has a yellow file folder in it, but there's only a few notes, no text and there were some tools too."

"Tools! Let me see." He reached for the backpack, but Robyn held it away.

Tattoo Guy scowled. "No more games. You don't know what you're dealing with here. I need that backpack. Now hand it over!" He made a menacing move toward her.

chapter five

Robyn's eyes glinted in defiance. "I will scream at the top of my lungs if you take one more step," she threatened. The university's Kinesiology building was still crowded with students. Tattoo Guy stopped. His eyeballs still bulged, but his face lost its expression of grim rage.

"Hey, I'm not going to hurt you." He sighed in exasperation. "Okay, look. If you check inside the small zippered pocket, you'll find a bright green snowboarding

sticker and a lift pass for Lake Louise. Right?"
He lifted one eyebrow as Robyn checked.

"Right," she said reluctantly.

She handed the backpack over. We watched
as the guy rummaged through the contents.
His lips pressed into a thin line when he saw
the variety of tools inside. "Some of the notes
are missing," he said.

"There was some brown powder too.
That, uh, kind of got spilled," I ventured.

Tattoo Guy frowned above his hairy
goatee.

"Was it...dangerous?" I asked.

Tattoo Guy snorted. "No. It was carob
powder. Totally harmless." He eyed us.
"Listen, was there anyone hanging around
when you found this?"

We shook our heads. "The hall was
empty," I said.

He nodded. Without another word, he
scooped up his sports equipment, balanced
the backpack in one arm and headed off
down the hall.

I shook my head. "Something very strange
is going on," I said.

"No kidding," said Robyn.

We walked down the corridor that led to the swimming pool. Nick, his wet hair standing up in damp spikes, was waiting outside the locker rooms with Nola. Nola kept her face deliberately averted from Nick.

Nick watched us approach with relief on his face.

"Looks like practice didn't go well," Robyn observed.

"Hey," I greeted him. "What's up?"

"I forgot my mom couldn't pick us up after practice. I'm supposed to carpool with *her*." Nick nodded in Nola's direction.

"Not the best option," I muttered.

"That's for sure," he said under his breath.

Robyn was already chatting with Nola. I was surprised to see her acting so friendly. I didn't think she liked Nola any better than we did.

"My dad's bringing the van," Nola said. "You guys can all fit in."

"That's great," Robyn gushed. "Nick

promised us pizza after he was finished practice. You want to come?"

Nick made a strangled noise, and from the look in his face, he was fighting the urge to kick Robyn in the shins.

Nola glanced in his direction. "Thanks, but I can't. I have tons of homework."

"Homework? In the summer?" I asked.

She gave me a brief look. "I'm in an accelerated program at school. I have to take a summer course. It's brutal." She picked up her swim bag. "We should go. My dad is probably here by now."

Outside we piled into Nola's van.

"Hi, kids." Her dad's tone was friendly as he pulled out into traffic. "Sorry it took me a little longer to get here—I had to see a student."

"So, Nola." Robyn worked hard to keep her voice casual. I could tell she was finally getting to the point. This had to be the reason she'd been cozying up to Nola. "I wanted to ask you some more about bio-piracy."

"Why?" Nola asked.

"I want to know more about it. I might be interested in joining your rally."

"Seriously?" Nola brightened right up. "Well, it started with this magazine article I read. It said people in other countries make remedies from plants or whatever they have around. Scientists are interested in that. So they send research teams to check out how the medicines work, whether they really do, stuff like that. Then in a few cases, the researchers, or the companies they work for, take out patents on the medicine."

"Why is that a problem?" Robyn asked.

"That means that no one else can make the remedy and sell it. So those companies make billions of dollars on a drug or a medicine that's been around for hundreds of years." Nola scowled fiercely. "Then, to make it even worse, the companies who produce the medicine go to these countries where the plants or trees naturally grow and take it all. They totally strip the land of them. It's the most unfair thing I've ever heard of. They take the right to make the medicines, and then they pirate the natural resources to make it."

"That's awful," Robyn said.

"Yeah." Nola shook her head. "If you want more information, you can look it up on the Internet. Just search *biological piracy* as the keywords. It'll all come up."

Nola's dad pulled up in front of Nick's house. "Thanks for the ride," Robyn and I said as we got out of the van. Nick joined us on the sidewalk.

"You guys coming in?" he said.

"In a minute," Robyn said, her voice tense. "I want to tell you guys something." She waved at Nola as the van pulled away.

"Hurry up, Robyn. It's starting to rain." Nick pulled the hood of his sweatshirt over his damp hair.

"I think Nola is behind the university's missing research!"

chapter six

"What? Robyn, you're crazy," I said as big raindrops pelted onto the sidewalk. This wasn't the greatest time to listen to another of Robyn's wild theories.

"I'm serious. I think Nola's been behind the missing research all along. She knows a lot about this bio-piracy thing. Don't you remember how she practically accused Meredith of holding back information that day at camp? I think she's so worked up about these countries getting stuff taken from them, she's prepared to do whatever it takes to make sure it doesn't happen."

"That's ridiculous," said Nick. "Nothing like that is going on at the university here."

"Maybe Nola thinks there is," Robyn answered.

I stared at her. "Even if she does, she's just a kid."

"So what? That could work in her favor. Who would suspect her?" Robyn said. "Remember how she argued with her dad that day in the van? He said the cancer research had something to do with plants. Nola probably thinks that means some other country's natural resources will end up getting pirated if the research goes through. What if she's trying to stop that from happening?"

"I think you're way out there on this one, Robyn. Just because Nola knows a lot about bio-piracy doesn't mean that she thinks it's happening here. Besides, that research had to do with cancer. That's pretty important. And you're suggesting that she'd steal from her own dad." I shook my head. "And what about Tattoo Guy? He's much more likely to be behind the missing research than Nola."

"Why?"

"Well, for one thing, we saw him moving boxes from the Faculty of Medicine into the basement of that house. What was in them? Why aren't they still at the university, if that's where they came from?" I said.

"There's another reason," Nick put in. "Money. If Nola said one thing that's right, it's that big drug companies would pay a lot of money for new research on drugs for cancer. If someone got ahold of that, they could make millions."

"We don't know that Tattoo Guy needs cash," Robyn said.

"Who doesn't?" I asked. "He looks like he could use it. And that vandalized backpack was his. It had research notes in it. Who knows what those were?"

"It could be someone else," Robyn argued. "If it's not Nola, then maybe it's someone we don't even know about, who really is in it for the money."

Nick glanced at both of us. "I say we check out Tattoo Guy first. It's time to get some answers."

"Ow! Robyn, you're kneeling on my finger!" I complained. The three of us had made plans to meet after supper. The rain had stopped, but the sky was still overcast and darker than usual, which was a lucky break for us. Our parents wanted us back home by nine thirty, and usually in August, it's still pretty light outside until nearly ten o'clock.

Robyn shuffled sideways, flattening herself into the mud underneath the bush at the side of Tattoo Guy's house. "Come on," she urged. She wiggled forward on her stomach.

One by one we slithered through the bushes, avoiding the motion-detector light attached to the garage. The gate was wood, with a heavy metal latch. Robyn slid it back, and the gate creaked gently open.

A block of light shone along the lawn. One of the basement windows was lit. Robyn motioned toward it.

"Be careful," I whispered. "If he catches us, we're toast. Especially after the backpack thing." The three of us crept cautiously forward.

A muffled click barely had time to register in my brain before I heard a familiar *putt-putt-putt* sound.

"Oh, no!" I said. "It's the—!" I was cut off as a spray of water hit me full in the face. It swung sideways, drenching Robyn and Nick before it arced over the rest of the lawn. "Automatic sprinkler system," I finished, wiping my face on my sleeve.

The soaker sprays blocked our way back to the gate. "This way," Nick said. We dashed across the backyard to the far corner and ducked behind a garden shed. By the time we got there, we were sopping.

"Brrrr." Robyn shivered. She wrung out the bottom of her jacket as a brisk breeze whistled along the fence. "Now what?"

Nick shook his hair like a dog after a bath. "I think those things are programmed to run for about twenty minutes. It should shut off soon."

"Who would be watering their lawn after a rainstorm anyway?" Robyn complained.

"Tattoo Guy probably just forgot to shut the system off. It doesn't look like anyone else is living here," I said.

We huddled behind the shed, growing colder and colder as the minutes wore on. Summer evenings in the foothills of the mountains can get pretty cool, and after our icy shower, I was about ready to swap my shorts and T-shirt for a parka.

"Can't we scrap this plan?" Nick gasped. "I mean, is this really worth it?"

"We might be talking about the cure for cancer, Nick," Robyn said. "Of course it's worth it. Besides, investigating Tattoo Guy was *your* idea."

"Wait." I held up one hand. "They're stopping." The noise of the sprinklers died away.

"Good." Robyn's teeth chattered. "Let's go!"

We snuck back over to the window, where the basement light was still on, and peered inside.

The room was sparsely furnished, with a desk and chair, a file cabinet and a long folding table against one wall. The table had a number of jars on it, each filled with varying amounts of some brownish liquid.

"Look, there are those dried bugs," Robyn whispered. She pointed to the baggie we'd found in the vandalized backpack.

"I don't think they're bugs," I said slowly.

"They're not," an angry voice said. The voice wasn't Nick's. It certainly wasn't Robyn's. Panic spurted through my veins. I made a scrambling move to escape, but a hand came down on my shoulder with the crushing grip of a steel vice.

chapter seven

"I think the three of you better come inside," he said grimly. I peered slowly upward and met the ferocious stare of the guy with the tattoo.

"No! Help! He's kidnapping us!" shrieked Robyn. Lights went on in the house next door. Nick, Robyn and I still crouched outside, by the basement window of Tattoo Guy's house.

"Whoa, whoa, whoa!" Tattoo Guy let go of me and held his hands up in surrender.

The three of us slowly stood up. "I'm not kidnapping anyone. But I want to know why you are sneaking around here at night. I thought dousing you with the sprinklers would get rid of you." He narrowed his eyes. "What are you up to?"

"I'd like to ask you the same thing," Robyn snapped. "What's going on in that basement, Frankenstein?"

I flinched at Robyn's gutsy response. This guy looked like he could eat us for breakfast, and she insisted on treating him like an older brother.

To my surprise, the guy laughed. "Fair enough." He glanced at Robyn's hunched, shivering frame. "Look, you're soaked. If you won't come in the house, at least come in the garage, out of the wind. I'll leave the garage door up."

"No way, Frankenstein." Robyn's teeth chattered.

"Actually the name's Finn Holt. *Not* Frankenstein." Tattoo Guy still looked amused.

"Finn?" Robyn questioned.

"Short for Finnigan." Something in his tone discouraged any jokes. "I can't let you kids freeze out here, but I really need to talk to you. Wait here." He strode around the corner of the house.

"Should we run?" Nick whispered.

"No way!" Robyn tossed her head. "I want to hear what he has to say."

Finn was back almost immediately. He handed us some weathered old blankets. They smelled kind of musty, but the heavy wool blocked the chill. Robyn snuggled into hers like she'd been rescued from the Arctic.

"They don't smell so good. Usually they're for the dog, but he's not here," Finn apologized. "The people who live here are gone for six months. I'm house-sitting."

"That's okay," I said.

"All right, Finn. Tell us. What's going on down there?" Nick said.

"I can't tell you." Finn smiled with the pleasantness of a piranha. "It's classified."

"We're going to find out anyway," Robyn said with determination. "You might as well just confess right now. We know a bunch of research has been stolen from the Faculty of Medicine, and that you're responsible."

"Wh-what?" Finn looked genuinely astonished. "You think *I* stole it?"

"Who else? The tooth fairy?" Robyn snapped.

"Is she for real?" Finn asked Nick and me.

We had to nod. "Yeah, she is," I said.

"Why would I steal my own research?" Finn asked.

"*Your* research?" Robyn said.

"Yeah, my research. They're my research notes that have gone missing. My backpack was stolen, and some of the stuff I was working on was inside. You guys should have figured that out—you were the ones who found it." He eyed us suspiciously. "Or took it. Who set you up for this? Did someone send you here tonight?"

I shook my head. "No. We had nothing to do with stealing that backpack."

Finn stared hard at me, then sighed. "I don't know whether to believe you or not. But if you suspect me and go blabbing to the police about my lab here and then the media shows up, then the secret's out anyway."

"Give us a reason not to suspect you, then," Robyn countered.

Finn hesitated for a long minute. "All right. This much I can tell you. I've been working on my PhD at the university. I've been doing research on the properties of the carob bean, since it has known benefits on liquid excrement from the large intestine."

Nick, Robyn and I looked at each other in confusion.

Finn noticed our blank expressions. "It's good for diarrhea," he explained.

Robyn stifled a laugh. "You're doing your doctorate on *diarrhea*?" she said.

"It can be a significant problem," Finn said stiffly. "In countries where people don't have access to good medical facilities, they can die from dysentery. Especially young children." Finn gave her an indignant glance. "So maybe it doesn't seem important to you, but just wait until the next time your butt's on the throne. Then we'll talk."

"Okay, okay. Keep going," I said. "What does that have to do with the missing research?"

"Well, I was experimenting. Those things you thought were bugs are actually carob pods. I was trying to isolate cells from the mature beans, and I found some interesting results when they were exposed to thermic response."

I felt my eyes glazing over. "What?"

"Never mind," Finn said impatiently. "I'm not telling you more than that. Whoever stole my notes knows that much anyway, but just in case you are spies, I'm not saying anything else. The point is, I found some of the isolated properties of carob had an increased regenerative ability—" He broke off as he looked at our faces. "Parts of the bean seemed to point toward helping rebuild damaged cells. I thought this might be a helpful part of cancer therapy, if I could develop it. But as soon as I confided my findings to my advisor, odd things started to happen. My notes were getting mixed up. Last month, some of my files went missing.

I lost my backpack twice before you found it vandalized. I think someone else has found out about what I'm doing. That's why I created a workplace here. I thought this would be a safe place to conduct my research—until you three showed up."

"Hmmm." I thought about this. Someone would have had to know about Finn's discovery in order to sabotage his work. "How did you let your advisor know about your findings?" I asked.

Finn shrugged. "E-mail."

"Did you send it to anyone else? Did your advisor?" I said.

"I think he forwarded it to one of the companies who helps with the cancer research. And of course, some of the other graduate students have teamed up with me. But they're one hundred percent reliable."

Nick and I shot each other a knowing glance. "It's out there then," Nick said. "Anyone who works there could have accessed it."

"Hackers could too, if they wanted to," I said. We needed to figure out who might have the information and start a new list of suspects. It was beginning to look like a big job.

"I doubt hackers could get into the system. It's pretty guarded," Finn answered.

"Why would anyone want your research?" Robyn wanted to know. "It's not like it's valuable, is it?"

Finn bristled. "It's very valuable. If someone could duplicate what I've been doing, there are pharmaceutical companies, especially in other countries, that would pay huge dollars for a new cancer drug. It could be worth billions—if it works. The problem is, I don't know that yet. I haven't finished working with it, let alone getting it into the testing process. Sometimes it takes years before a drug can be approved for public use."

"So, someone could sell the recipe for the drug privately and make a lot of money," Robyn surmised.

"Yeah. Totally," Finn said.

"What about if someone wanted to prevent companies from going into countries where the carob bean grows and taking all the carob?" asked Robyn.

"I suppose that could be a reason too," Finn said. "Carob is fairly common...I don't know." He shook his head. "All I know is that I have to present my findings to my senior advisor next Tuesday, and someone is making things very difficult for me."

Robyn nodded grimly. "And I have an idea who it is."

chapter eight

"Explain to me again why we're here," Robyn said as the bus pulled away from the curb in a puff of exhaust. I looked up at the enormous hospital complex that housed the Cancer Research Center. "When we know that our chief suspect is Nola."

"Oh, come on, Robyn. It's not Nola," Nick said. Summer day camp had finished, and I'd persuaded Nick and Robyn to spend the day investigating. "Stealing research is way too complicated for a kid to pull off."

"Oh, really?" Robyn folded her arms across her chest. "Finn said someone stole his backpack *twice*. That's all anyone had to do to get some of his notes. A kid could do that, easy. We're not talking about breaking into a high-tech lab."

"How would she even know about Finn's research?" Nick argued. "It's not like he advertised that he was trying to develop a cancer treatment."

"Her dad is a professor, remember?" Robyn retorted.

"He could be in a totally different department," said Nick.

Robyn frowned. "No, he said he works in the Faculty of Medicine. He could easily have information about Finn's research."

"Look, you guys, we're here because we need to find a connection between the missing research and whoever took it, whether it's Nola or someone else," I said. "Finn's not off the hook either. He says it was his research that was stolen, but how do we really know that? He could have been feeding us a major line. I found that business card from Seaton Pharmaceuticals in the backpack. If he's testing for a new drug treatment, why would he have a card from a company like that, unless he was planning to sell his research?"

Robyn and Nick glanced at me. "I don't know," Nick said.

"I don't know either," I said. "And this is the only place I can think of that might have the answers."

"But, Trevor," Robyn protested. "We don't even know what we're looking for."

"Anything," I said. "There was no address listed for Seaton on the card, but I think people around here might have heard of them. We'll start asking some questions and keep our eyes open."

"Speaking of opening your eyes, look who's over there," said Robyn.

I looked where Robyn was pointing. A dark-haired woman was standing near a park bench, laughing with an older woman. It was Meredith. I didn't know the older woman. She could have been anywhere between thirty and fifty years old, she was so rail-thin and haggard. Her head was covered with a knitted toque, and she wore a thick coat, even though it was warm. Meredith smiled, breaking off her conversation as we approached. "Well, if it isn't my star campers," she said. "Trevor, how's the robot development going?"

I felt the tips of my ears turn red. "I've given up robots," I mumbled. "Too dangerous."

Meredith grinned. "Trevor nearly turned a mild-mannered robot into a nuclear explosion in my class," she explained to the older woman.

The woman turned kind eyes on me. "Never mind. Sometimes accidents lead to wonderful discoveries when it comes to science. That's what experiments are about, right?"

I nodded. The woman turned back to Meredith. "Well, I'd better go. I have a hot date with a radiation machine." She shuffled off in the direction of the Cancer Treatment Center. Meredith watched her go, her face thoughtful. She held a half-empty cup of coffee in one hand.

"It's really sad," she muttered.

"What's sad?" Robyn asked.

"People like her need every advancement we can give them."

"Isn't she getting that?" Nick said.

Meredith nodded. "Of course she is. But there might be new research, new findings, that could help. She can't afford to wait for years until a new treatment is approved. She needs it now."

Robyn was puzzled. "But you told Nola at camp that new treatments had to go through strict testing to make sure that they worked."

"That's right," Meredith agreed. "They do. But when it comes to cancer, people are willing to take a chance. They don't have time to wait. Why not try something, if it could help save your life?"

"Because it could be dangerous," Robyn whispered. Meredith had turned away, tossing her coffee cup in the trash.

"Gotta go back to work, kids," she said, stifling a yawn.

"Work?" I asked.

"Yeah. As in, earning money." A scowl creased Meredith's face. "I'm back at my old job, working mornings here."

"You are?" Robyn asked. "I thought you'd be getting ready for school. The master's program is a pretty big deal, isn't it?"

"Yeah." Meredith's voice sounded odd. "Well, see you kids around."

We watched her go.

"Well, that was an interesting coincidence," Robyn commented.

I stopped. When it came to crime, anything that seemed like a coincidence usually wasn't. "Let's follow her," I said.

"What? Why?" asked Robyn.

"I don't know. I just think we should. It's a bit weird, us running into her. Let's see where she goes."

The three of us ambled after her. We watched her enter a nearby building. After a couple of moments, we followed her through the large glass doors, just in time to see her step on the elevator.

"Wait," I whispered, my eyes fastened on the digital numbers that displayed each floor the elevators stopped on. "Let see where she gets off."

"We'll lose her," Nick argued. "We don't know if she was alone in the elevator."

But the elevator made only one stop before it began to descend.

"Fifth floor," I said. "Come on, let's go." We jumped into a second elevator, pushed the button and began to rise. When the elevator doors opened, we poked our heads out cautiously.

The hallway was empty. Several doors had nameplates on them, but only one caught my eye. The door at the end had fancy lettering that clearly spelled out the words *Seaton Pharmaceuticals*.

chapter nine

"Finn!" I pounded on the front door of his house. "Finn!"

The door opened. Finn stood there, bleary-eyed, his hair standing out in a wild halo around his head. Clearly he had been sleeping. "What? What's the matter?"

"Do you know a woman named Meredith? She's in the graduate program. She probably works with you."

Finn blinked. "Huh?"

Nick came to my rescue. "She's a student.

She has dark hair and really blue eyes. She was our day-camp instructor. She told us she was applying to the graduate studies program in the Faculty of Medicine."

Finn shook his head as if to clear it. "Sorry, guys. This isn't making sense to me. I was up most of the night, trying to replicate the missing research. What's going on with Meredith?"

"You know her, then?" Robyn said eagerly.

"Yeah, I know her. Sort of. We went out for coffee a few times. I asked her out after that, but she said no. And that day after Trevor caught me sneaking around her office, she really told me off."

I thought back to how Finn had scared me that day. "What were you doing there?" I asked.

"Looking for my research notes. At first I thought I'd lost them. I figured I should check all the places I'd been, and that included Meredith's office."

"So why didn't you just walk in there?"

"And look like a dork? Get real, Trevor.

I wasn't about to confess that I thought I lost six month's worth of research after the girl shut me down."

"So, what made you think the research was stolen? Maybe you really did lose it," Nick said.

Finn shook his head. "No. I had my backpack disappear twice, remember? I never found the first one. There wasn't anything much in it, so that didn't matter. You guys found the second one. It didn't get ripped like that by itself. Someone was after what I had inside."

"How much did they get?" asked Robyn. "Was all your research in there?"

"Not all of it," Finn answered. "They took my notes on procedures, but the findings weren't complete. I usually keep most of the important stuff in the lab. That's why I moved it here to the house."

"Okay. Back to Meredith. How much does she know about your research? Has she been working with you in the graduate studies program at the university? Have you ever heard of a company called Seaton Pharmaceuticals?" I peppered him with questions.

Finn held up one hand. "Whoa! Wait a second. The only thing I know about Seaton is that they have a research arm that works with the university on a contract basis."

"Do they sell the drugs after they're developed?" I asked.

"I really don't know." Finn shrugged. "But they would have contacts with corporations that do, most likely. Why?"

"We found a Seaton Pharmaceuticals business card with your stuff the day your backpack was vandalized," I said.

Finn looked completely mystified. "I have no idea how it got there. I've never dealt with them."

Nick, Robyn and I exchanged glances. "Meredith works there. She could be passing information off to them," said Nick.

"She could be," Finn answered slowly. "If she had access to the information."

"What do you mean?" I asked.

"She never made it into the graduate

studies program. They rejected her application."

"It has to be Meredith," I said. The three of us were walking to Robyn's from Finn's house. "She's hanging around the university, but she doesn't even go to school there. And she just happened to show up when Robyn and I found Finn's backpack."

"She could have just stumbled on it, like we did," Robyn said.

"In the basement of the Kinesiology building?" I scoffed. "Not likely."

"She said she had a locker down there," Robyn argued.

"Why would she have a locker at the university if she doesn't even go to school there?" I countered. "She has to be lying."

"Well, she could have registered for one, since she had planned to be there," Robyn said. "She was working for the day camps too."

I shook my head. "I doubt they hand out lockers unless you have a current student ID."

Robyn and Nick were silent.

"What's the matter with you two? Meredith is a really strong suspect!" I said.

"Well, I was just thinking," Nick answered. "We still don't know much about Finn. All we have is what he's telling us. How do we know he isn't passing the information himself? He could sell the research for a lot of money. He could be lying to us about his connections with Seaton. He might even be working *with* Meredith."

I shook my head. "You're forgetting Finn's vandalized backpack. Why would he trash his own stuff? The fact that Meredith was there is too much of a coincidence."

"And I was thinking that you guys are forgetting Nola," Robyn said.

Nick rolled his eyes. "Robyn, let's get real. Nola would never be able to sell the research."

"No. But that's not why she would've taken it. She would have destroyed it," said Robyn. "*Think*, you guys. Finn said that he was researching properties of the *carob bean*. Where does carob grow?"

"I have no idea," I answered.

"Well, I do. I looked it up." Robyn dug a folded paper out of her jeans pocket and handed it to me. It was a printout from an Internet site. "It grows in warm climates, like the Mediterranean, North Africa and desert areas in South America. Nola's hyper-vigilant about this bio-piracy thing. You can bet that if she thought a company like Seaton was about to make big money by pirating carob from the countries where it grows, she'd be all over that. Of course she'd take the research!"

"But we have no way to prove that she knew anything about what Finn was working on, remember?" Nick argued.

"She would if her dad is Finn's advisor," retorted Robyn.

"So how are you going to find that out?" I asked.

"It's not hard," Robyn said. She produced her cell phone. "One phone call should do it." She dialed Information and got the number of the university switchboard, then called the number. "Yes, I'm looking for Dr. Pierce's office in the Faculty of Medicine." She tilted the phone toward us, so we could hear the tinny music as she waited on hold.

A male voice answered, "Dr. Pierce."

"Dr. Pierce, this is Robyn, Nola's friend," Robyn said.

"Yes?"

"I have a message for you from one of your doctorate students, Finnigan Humphmm." We didn't know Finn's last name. I grinned as Robyn mumbled something indecipherable.

"Finn? Yes, is everything okay?" Dr. Pierce immediately sounded concerned.

"Oh, yeah. His cell phone ran out of batteries, that all. And he had to go somewhere, so I said I'd call and let you know that he'd be a few minutes late for your meeting this afternoon."

"This afternoon? We're not scheduled to meet today."

"Oh. He must have gotten that mixed up. I'll let him know. Thanks, Dr. Pierce." Robyn hung up and smiled in triumph. "He's definitely Finn's advisor. If that isn't proof, I don't know what is!"

Nick and I glanced at one another. I couldn't tell what he was thinking.

"Dr. Pierce might not have any idea what Nola's up to," Robyn said finally.

"Finn's backpack could've just been stolen. Stuff probably gets ripped off all the time. Maybe it had nothing to do with the research at all," Nick added.

"You guys! You're building cases here that we don't really need. I still think it's Meredith," I said.

"I think it's Nola." Robyn folded her arms across her chest.

"I have to say, I still think it could be Finn," said Nick.

"Augh!" I wanted to tear my hair out. "We have to get some proof. The only thing we know for sure is that Finn is presenting the research to Dr. Pierce next Tuesday. Whoever is behind the theft has to act before that, or it will be too late. Dr. Pierce and Finn's research team can claim they discovered it first."

Nick nodded. "You're right. There has to be a way to set a trap to get the proof we need."

"Yeah," I answered. "But how?"

chapter ten

"We're running out of time, you guys," said Robyn as we walked home Monday afternoon. The deadline was tomorrow. Finn was going to present his findings in the morning, and we still didn't have a plan.

"Tell me something I don't know," I answered glumly.

"I still think Seaton Pharmaceuticals has something to do with the whole thing. It's no coincidence that Meredith works there and we found a Seaton business card in Finn's backpack," said Nick.

"Yeah, but you think that Finn's selling his own research, and he didn't seem to know much about Seaton," I said.

"I know. But we have to start somewhere." Nick shrugged.

Robyn stopped. She pointed in the direction of Finn's place, just a few houses down the street from the school. "Look, you guys."

I looked. Nola was marching up the driveway.

"What's *she* doing *there*?" Robyn said.

"Good question," I said. The three of us froze, watching.

Robyn's eyes narrowed. "Let's find out."

The three of us crept closer and ducked behind the shrubbery in the neighbor's yard. We could see Nola climb the front steps and ring the doorbell. Finn opened the door. Nola reached into her pocket and handed him a bunch of folded bills. I nearly fell over when I realized what it was.

"She's giving him money!" Robyn hissed.

"Shh, I can't hear." I tried to edge closer, the evergreen bush raking my face. I strained to hear what Nola was saying.

"Thanks, Finn. Your notes were the key to the whole thing," Nola said.

"So everything worked out?" Finn asked.

Nola smiled. "Yeah. It went great." She waved as she started down the steps. "See ya."

The three of us flattened ourselves to the ground. Why was Nola paying Finn off? Could she be involved after all? Robyn was sure Nola was the culprit, and she'd just mentioned using Finn's notes...

Nola strode past where we were hidden and turned down the street toward the school. As soon as she was safely out of sight, I stood up and brushed myself off.

"I told you it was Nola!" Robyn crowed in triumph. "That pretty much proves it."

"Except for one thing," said Nick. "Your whole theory is based on the idea that Nola would destroy the research, not sell it. So why would she be giving Finn money?"

Robyn frowned.

"Good point," I said. "I think the next step is to do our own research—on Seaton Pharmaceuticals."

At my house, I clicked the computer mouse. I was sandwiched between Nick and Robyn as the three of us shared my dad's office chair and stared at the screen. A bright revolving graphic filled the page, stretching out to form the company's name. "This is it," I said. We'd found Seaton's web page.

"Click there," Robyn said, pointing to a heading titled *What's New*. I guided the mouse and brought up the page.

I scanned the text. It talked about new drug treatments that Seaton had developed. There was no mention of anything suspicious, until I scrolled down to the very bottom of the page. Then it said that Seaton was proud to be involved in cutting-edge research on a promising new drug treatment for various types of cancer.

"Look at that." Nick pointed to the same paragraph I'd just read.

"It has to be Finn's research," Robyn said.

"Maybe," I said. "At least we know Seaton is on board with the cancer research, but we have no way to know for sure that this is Finn's."

"Oh, come on, Trevor!" Robyn scoffed. "What more do you need? Research for a new cancer drug gets ripped off, and suddenly this company is advertising a promising new treatment? Of course it's Finn's."

"Other people are researching cancer too, you know," I argued. "There could be other drugs in development. This web site doesn't say anything about carob beans. Finn's research deals with carob."

"Run it, then," Nick said. "Maybe we'll find a link."

I typed in carob bean. At first the search engine pulled up sites for herbal remedies. I clicked on one, which gave us a picture of the bean pods and a description of what carob was used for. Just like Finn had told us, carob was useful for diarrhea. I backtracked and scrolled through the rest of the search engine's listing. There was a blog entry that mentioned carob in the opening sentences. The word *Seaton* appeared lower down, in the blogger's web address.

Nick and Robyn stared at me, wide-eyed. "We've got it," I said, my voice hoarse.

"Double-click." Robyn held her breath.

The computer whirred softly. Then an error message came up. *The page cannot be found*, it said.

"Augh! I don't believe it!" Robyn burst out. The three of us groaned in disappointment.

"Someone's removed it from the web." Nick frowned. "It probably wasn't supposed to be on there in the first place."

"But now we know. Seaton's connected. Someone's made contact with them about the carob beans," I said.

"Which means," Robyn speculated, "that someone plans to sell them Finn's research before Finn presents it tomorrow morning."

Nick glanced at his watch. "Their office is closed by now. But first thing tomorrow morning, how much do you want to bet Nola, Finn or Meredith shows up at Seaton to complete the sale?"

I shut the computer down. "Then that's where we'll be too, to catch them in the act!"

chapter eleven

Robyn stifled a yawn. "Didn't your parents think it was a bit weird that Trevor and I wanted to come to a six AM swim practice?"

"Yeah. They thought you were nuts." Nick grinned.

The rest of the university campus still slumbered in the early morning, but the Kinesiology building was brightly lit, already a hub of activity.

My eyelids felt sandy with sleep and a

huge yawn nearly dislocated my jaw. "We'd better get going. Meredith said she starts work early, and we need to get there before any of our suspects show up."

Nick shouldered his swim bag. "This way. There's an exit on the other end of the building. I don't want Nola or anyone else from the swim team to see me cutting out."

"Will you get in trouble for skipping practice?" Robyn asked.

"I don't know. Hopefully the coach will think that preventing the sale of stolen cancer research is worth missing practice for," answered Nick.

"He will," I answered confidently.

Nick pushed open the heavy glass door that led outside. The three of us hurried down the street. It was quiet—only the distant noise of traffic broke the stillness.

"Let's go," I whispered.

We broke into a jog. Within a few minutes we were off campus and headed toward the cancer research facility. Another twenty minutes or so, and we were looking at the light shining from the windows of the big office building. I tried to remember exactly where Seaton Pharmaceuticals was—there were a lot of other offices inside the complex.

"They probably have security," Nick said.

Several women were approaching the building from the parking lot. I nudged Robyn and gestured to them. She nodded. "Come on," she whispered.

We tagged behind them as they went inside the unlocked front door. The women went straight to the elevator, not even paying attention to us. We headed for the stairs.

"People must start work really early around here," commented Robyn.

"It's not so early now. It's almost seven o'clock," I said.

We ran up several flights of stairs, closing the door to the stairwell gently behind us as we reached the fifth floor.

The silence of the huge building settled around us. All the office doors were shut—except one. The door to Seaton Pharmaceuticals was propped wide open.

Great, I thought. But then I saw the secretary sitting at the wide, granite-topped reception desk. I could see several dark leather armchairs through the window next to the door. A glass table between the chairs had business magazines stacked neatly next to a floral arrangement of twigs and greenery.

"Rats." Robyn frowned. "Secretaries aren't supposed to start work until later."

"Maybe she has something extra to do," I said.

Nick checked his watch. "Practice is nearly over now. If Nola has anything to do with this, she should be here soon."

"And if it's Finn, he should be arriving any minute," Robyn added. "He has to have time to talk with these people before his appointment with Dr. Pierce."

The minutes ticked by. We huddled near the elevators, out of the secretary's line of sight. Nobody showed up, not Finn, or Nola or Meredith. I was getting antsy.

"If we could get inside Meredith's office, we might find the proof we need," Robyn said.

"Yeah, but how are we going to get past her?" I gestured toward the secretary.

That question was answered as she got up and strode out into the hall.

"Hide!" I croaked. I shoved Nick and Robyn into the nearest doorway as silently as possible. I wedged myself against a large flowerpot nearby, doing my best impression of a potted palm. Lucky for us, the secretary didn't look our way. Looking slightly sick, she hesitated, but then made a beeline for the bathroom without waiting to shut the office door.

"Quick! Let's go," I said, as soon as the washroom door had shut behind her.

"You guys, wait!" Nick whispered. "It's one thing to stake out the outside of an office and wait until someone shows up. It's totally different to sneak inside. It's private property. We could get in deep trouble for this!"

"Look, Nick. This is no time to chicken out," Robyn snapped. "If we don't find that research now, it's going to be too late. So, what's more important? Saving what could the most important cure ever for mankind, or worrying about a little thing like trespassing?" Robyn didn't wait for an answer. She dashed inside, ducked around the secretary's desk and headed for the nearest office.

"A *little thing* like trespassing?" Nick looked at me. I shrugged as we hurried to catch up to her. "I knew I should have gone to swim practice," Nick muttered.

The three of us snuck down the hall behind the receptionist desk. The office doors were all open, ready for the workday. So far, there was no sign of anyone else.

"How will we know which desk is Meredith's?" Robyn whispered.

"Look for something personal. A photo, a nameplate, business card, whatever," I answered.

"This is the wrong office. Let's try the next one," Nick said.

We crept down the hallway. In the next office, I spotted a photo of Meredith leaning against a tree, holding a puppy. "Bingo!" I said.

The desk was littered with papers and several yellow file folders.

Yellow file folders.

My brain suddenly clicked on. There had been a yellow file folder on Meredith's desk at summer camp, the day Finn had been searching for his lost research. There had also been a yellow file folder in Finn's vandalized backpack. Why hadn't I made that connection before?

I opened the folders. They were full of notes on various experiments, but I couldn't tell if they were written in Finn's handwriting or Meredith's.

"Take these." I stuffed them inside Nick's swim bag.

"What are you doing!" Robyn exclaimed in a horrified whisper. She pulled the folders right back out of Nick's bag. "You can't just take papers out of someone's office!"

"They might be evidence, maybe even part of the stolen research. I can't tell for sure. We'll have to ask Finn," I said.

"But what if it's not the research! That's stealing," Robyn countered. "We should photocopy them."

"We don't have time." I rubbed my forehead. "The secretary's going to be back any second."

Nick crept to the door and peered out. "She's still gone," he whispered, returning to the desk. "And anyway," Nick added. "Isn't secretly photocopying something just as bad as stealing?"

"If these notes are what we think they are, it proves that Meredith is guilty. We need to show the police," I argued.

Robyn thought fast. The deep file drawer of the desk wasn't quite closed. She yanked the drawer open, grabbed the yellow folders and stuffed them way in the back, behind some files that were overflowing with paper. "There," she said. "That way we haven't taken it, but if it *is* the stolen research, we know exactly where to tell the police to find it." She slammed the drawer shut.

The movement jiggled the computer

mouse. The screensaver disappeared, replaced with a plain blue screen cluttered with icons. One window was still open.

"She left her e-mail up," Nick said under his breath.

The e-mail server was the type that showed the text of the first e-mail in the queue. It was right in plain sight—we didn't even have to snoop. The message had been received less than ten minutes ago. It said:

> *Meredith,*
> *Very interested in your previous message. Would be interested in discussing your findings on properties of carob later this morning. Will phone to confirm time.*
>
> *John Wingle*
> *President*
> *Seaton Pharmaceuticals*

"Holy crabgrass, Batman," Nick said. "It's from Mr. Big himself."

"She's the one. This confirms it," I said, just as the phone gave a sudden ring. Our nerves were so on edge, the shrill sound sent us diving for cover.

We waited in tense silence as the rings stopped. There was a short pause, then Meredith's voice mail came through the speaker on the phone.

"Hi, you've reached Meredith Gorden at Seaton Pharmaceuticals. I will be away from the office during the morning of Tuesday, August 25. Please leave me a message, and I will return your call as soon as I can." *Beep*! The machine shut off.

"They didn't leave a message," Robyn observed, standing up and brushing her jeans off.

"Meredith won't be in the office this morning," I said slowly. "That doesn't make sense. She needs to present the research to the president this morning, before Finn can give it Dr. Pierce."

"Finn and Nola didn't show up either," Robyn said.

"Of course they didn't," Nick scoffed.

"The e-mail proves that Meredith is guilty."

"Unless she's doing her own research on carob beans," Robyn countered. "Finn said the findings weren't complete when they disappeared."

Every cell in my body froze. *The findings weren't complete when they disappeared.*

"How could we be so stupid!" I yelped.

"What are you talking about?" Robyn stared at me as I leaped up.

"The findings weren't complete. Meredith doesn't have all the research she needs. That's why she's not at work this morning!" I fought down the urge to panic. "We're in the wrong place!"

chapter twelve

I raced out of Meredith's office, Nick and Robyn on my heels. "We're never going to make it in time!" I said. The secretary stared at us openmouthed, as we dashed past her desk and out the door of the Seaton Pharmaceuticals office.

"Where are we going?" Robyn gasped, as we ran past the elevators. I yanked the stairwell door open and clattered down the steps at top speed.

"Don't you get it?" I answered. "Meredith

doesn't have all the findings she needs. She has to get the final research before she can give it to the president of Seaton Pharmaceuticals. She's probably at Finn's house right now!"

"You think she'll break in?" Nick asked.

"Yeah, I do. If this research is worth as much money to Seaton as I think it is, Meredith won't let a detail like breaking and entering get in her way." I opened the door at the bottom of the stairwell and blasted through the lobby. "Come on. We have to get out of here."

"How?" Robyn hollered as I ran up the street.

"The bus!" I yelled back. "Head for the university. That bus stop is on the closest route to Finn's house!" My sneakers pounded on the sidewalk. I ran until I thought my feet would drop off.

"Trevor, it'll take forever on the bus," Robyn wheezed as we neared the Kinesiology building. We had to pass it to get to the bus stop.

"You're right. How much cash do you have?" I said. "We could get a cab."

Nick hunted in the pocket of his jeans. "Fifty cents," he said.

Robyn snorted. "Cabs are expensive. Besides, we'd still have to wait until it gets here. We need to leave *now*." She looked at Nick. "How did you tell your mom you were getting home after practice?"

"Carpooling with Nola," Nick answered.

"Has she already gone?" asked Robyn.

Nick checked his watch. "Probably. Practice was over twenty minutes ago."

But at that moment, Nola walked out of the building. Robyn raced up to her.

"Nola, could your dad give us a ride?" she blurted.

"To Nick's house?" Nola asked. She narrowed her gaze at him. "Why weren't you at practice anyway?"

"No, to mine." Robyn glanced at me. Finn's house backed onto the same park area as Robyn's. If Nola's dad could get us to Robyn's house, it would be a matter of minutes to run to Finn's place.

"Would that be okay?" Robyn said, her voice tense.

Nola shrugged. "I guess so. But what's the big deal?"

Nobody knew how to answer. "I...just really have to get home fast," Robyn said. "It's important."

"No problem," said Nola. "Dad should be waiting for me by the parking lot. He has to hurry though. He has a meeting he has to get back to."

Robyn, Nick and I exchanged glances. We knew why Dr. Pierce had to be back— he was supposed to meet with Finn about Finn's research on carob beans, *if* Meredith didn't get to it first.

We broke into a run, reaching the parking lot in record time. Dr. Pierce opened the van door.

"Can you drop Robyn, Trevor and Nick off too, Dad?" Nola asked.

"Sure, hop in," Dr. Pierce answered. We climbed in, and Dr. Pierce edged the van into traffic. Would we get there in time? I stared out the window. Robyn chewed on her thumbnail. Nick tapped his fingers against his thigh. No one spoke. The streets slid past.

"You guys all right?" Nola said at last.

"Yeah," I said.

"Fine," Robyn answered.

"Mmph," grunted Nick.

Nola frowned. "You still never said why you didn't make it to practice, Nick," she whispered. "What's the matter? Quitting already?"

"Not now, Nola. Back off, okay?" Nick said through gritted teeth. The traffic light changed. We were close now—I craned my neck as we passed Finn's street, but I couldn't see anything unusual. Dr. Pierce pulled the van up in front of Robyn's house. We piled out.

As Dr. Pierce drove away, Robyn and I sped off down the street, Nick right behind us. We turned down Finn's street.

"Trevor, wait," Robyn panted. "We need to catch Meredith red-handed. We can't just go barging in there."

I slowed down. "You're right." We crept ɔ the side of the house. "Look," I whispered, pointing to a trail of wet footprints that led to Finn's backyard. The morning felt warm and fresh, the grass was heavy with dew.

"Come on," Robyn said. The three of us tiptoed in the same direction as the footprints. Softly, I released the gate latch. Nick, Robyn and I edged toward the basement window, where we had caught our first glimpse of Finn's lab.

The window was wide open.

A scraping noise followed by a thump made us flatten ourselves against the wall of the house. I winced as the corner of the sprinkler control box jabbed me in the back. I forgot the pain instantly as a black duffel bag was tossed out the window. A hand appeared, grasping the window frame, followed by an elbow.

I held my breath. The rest of Meredith wiggled through the narrow window. She paused, her hips balanced on the window frame, her hands braced in the damp soil beside the house. She glanced sideways and saw us squeezed together like upright sardines. Her eyes widened, and she scrambled the rest of the way out the window, grabbing the duffel bag.

What now? I realized in that moment that I had no plan. I tensed. Meredith sensed the hesitation and put on a smile.

"Hey, guys," she greeted us.

She slung the duffel bag over her shoulder and wiped her muddy hands on the back of her jeans.

"What's going on, Meredith?" Robyn's gaze was steady. She took a step forward, folding her arms across her chest.

Meredith gave a short laugh. "Looks peculiar, I know. I used to go out with Finn, and I left some stuff at his place. He wasn't too happy when I told him I didn't want to see him anymore. Climbing in the window was the only way to get my things back."

For half a second, I wanted to believe her. She just didn't look like a crook. But then I saw the corner of a bright yellow file folder poking out the open zipper of the duffel bag, and I knew the truth.

"You're a great liar, Meredith, but it won't work," I said. "We know what you've been doing. You left your e-mail up in your office. We saw a message from the president of Seaton Pharmaceuticals on your computer. Too bad you weren't at work today—it seems your boss is very interested in Finn's research on carob beans and cancer."

Meredith narrowed her eyes. "Really? And who gave you the right to sneak into my office?"

"Who gave you the right to steal important cancer research?" Robyn snapped.

"Is that what you think I'm doing?" Meredith's jaw tightened. "Listen, little girl, there are people who are dying. They need this research, and they need it now. Not in two years when it's gone through all the red tape."

"The red tape is there for a reason," I retorted. "They have to test drugs to make sure they're safe. You even said that yourself."

"Yeah, well, I lied. I changed my mind about that when my sister got diagnosed," Meredith said bitterly.

"What?" I said.

"My sister." Meredith gave me a twisted smile. "You met her, that day in front of the building. She was diagnosed a few months ago. Cancer. Terminal. You think I'm going to sit back and wait for the political garbage to get sorted out? You think that if I can expedite the process, I won't? You think I won't help her if I can?"

Horrified, the three of us stared at her. Nick was the first to recover. "But you can't say you won't make a nice profit from selling it," Nick added.

"So what? The university had a chance to have me on their research team. They blew it. They turned me down. Any money I make off this is justified," said Meredith.

"I don't think so," I said grimly. "What you're doing is wrong, Meredith. You could be harming your sister even more than the cancer is, if the drug is produced before it's safe."

Meredith expression quivered for a fraction of a second, then hardened. "What do you know? You're just a kid."

"Hand over the duffel bag," I demanded.

"Hah. In your dreams, Trevor." Meredith clutched the duffel bag and took off across the backyard toward the other gate.

"Quick! Stop her!" Robyn yelled.

My thoughts collided. In an instant, I had a plan. I swung around to the sprinkler control box that had just put a permanent dent in my back. I ripped the door open, cranked the control to max, and hit the power switch. Finn had trapped us the same way a few weeks ago and obviously hadn't shut the system off.

The familiar ticking was broken only by the solid swish of water. It hit Meredith full in the face just before she reached the back fence.

I took off running and grabbed the back of Meredith's jacket, reaching for the duffel bag. She turned on me like a wildcat, squirming out of my grasp. "Not this time," she said, through gritted teeth. "I've worked way too hard to be stopped now." She swung the duffel bag in the direction of my head. I ducked, but Meredith's shriek of dismay made me look up. The yellow file folder had flown out of the bag and landed on the now-soggy lawn, spilling the sheaf of notes over the grass. The sprinkler instantly soaked it, sending the ink running down the papers in streams of blue. Within seconds the notes were completely unreadable.

"They're ruined!" Meredith cried. She sank down on her knees and scrabbled frantically through the wet paper for anything that could be saved. The paper disintegrated into mushy clumps. Meredith held the squishy pieces in her hands, a look of sick horror on her face. "You idiot!" she shouted at me. "You've just destroyed what could have been a cure for thousands of people!"

"Not quite." The sprinkler system suddenly shut off, and Finn strode across the yard. He folded his arms and glared down at Meredith. Sirens could be heard in the distance. "I figured you might try to steal the final research, Meredith. I wasn't born yesterday, you know." He smiled pleasantly, just as two police cruisers pulled up to the front of the house. "What you had in that file folder was the Latin translation of a recipe for chocolate chip cookies!"

chapter thirteen

I watched as the police car pulled away from the curb with Meredith inside. She refused to look out the window. Stone-faced, she stared straight ahead. The car turned a corner and disappeared from view.

Finn ran a hand through his wild bushy hair and sighed. Nola spoke up. She'd asked her dad to let her stay at Robyn's, followed us to Finn's and stayed hidden until just before Meredith was arrested.

"So that's why Nick missed practice," she said.

It was such a know-it-all Nola-type thing to say that I started to laugh. She frowned indignantly, which made me laugh harder.

Robyn looked at her watch. "Finn, how are you ever going to present your research to Dr. Pierce by ten o'clock? You have five minutes to get all the way across town!"

"It's all right," Finn assured her. "I talked to Nola's dad already. Dr. Pierce said I could reschedule the meeting for later today. There's no rush now that Meredith has been caught. No one can scoop my findings and give them to anyone else, including Seaton Pharmaceuticals."

"Good." Robyn breathed a sigh of relief, but then a look of realization crossed her face.

I had the same thought. It was the one detail that we hadn't figured out yet. "How come Nola was giving you money?" I asked Finn. "We saw her come up to the house and hand you a wad of cash."

"Why do you want to know?" replied Finn.

"Because it doesn't make sense," I said. "When we saw her pay you, Nola said that your notes were the key to the whole thing. Then you asked her if everything worked out. Nola is so against biological piracy. Since you were researching carob beans which grow in other countries, we figured she was involved somehow." I paused as Finn stifled a laugh.

Nola giggled. "Trust me. I had nothing to do with any of it."

"So what's going on?" I demanded.

Nola faced us. "Finn's my tutor. I told you guys I was in the accelerated program at school. Well, it's a lot harder than I thought it would be. My dad suggested I ask Finn if he could help me study for the science class I'm taking over the summer."

"And I'm a student, man. Any cash is good," Finn added. "So I was happy to help."

It all made sense now. Nola cleared her throat. "I followed you guys when you took off, and you're lucky I did. When I saw Trevor trying to get the files away from Meredith, I ran and got Finn, and then he phoned the police. Technically, I saved your butts."

I rolled my eyes. It was just like Nola to take the credit.

"So I want to know which one of you plans to explain all this to the news, because there are four reporters and two camera crews out there." Nola pointed toward the street.

"What!" I peered around the bushes. News vans were parked by the curb, and several people were milling around on the driveway.

"I guess the call over the police scanner sounded interesting," Nick commented. "Think about it...break and enter in progress, stolen research, three teenage kids assaulting woman with sprinkler system...I can hear it all now."

I groaned.

Finn answered. "I'll talk to them," he said. "But when they hear about all this, there's no way they'll believe it!"

This is Michele Martin Bossley's third book in the Orca Currents series. The previous two, *Swiped* and *Cracked* also feature Trevor, Robyn and Nick. Michele lives in Calgary, Alberta.